July 15 2018

20,000 Leagues Under the Sea

*Retold from the Jules Verne
original by Lisa Church*

Illustrated by Dan Andreasen

STERLING CHILDREN'S BOOKS

New York

STERLING CHILDREN'S BOOKS
New York

An Imprint of Sterling Publishing Co., Inc.
1166 Avenue of the Americas
New York, NY 10036

Text © 2006 by Lisa Church
Illustrations © 2006 by Dan Andreasen

Classic Starts is a trademark of Sterling Publishing Co., Inc.

ISBN 978-1-4027-2533-3

Library of Congress Cataloging-in-Publication Data

Church, Lisa R., 1960–
  20,000 leagues under the sea: retold from the Jules Verne original / abridged by Lisa Church;
illustrated by Dan Andreasen ; afterword by Arthur Pober.
    p. cm.—(Classic starts)
Summary: The abridged adventures of a French professor and his two companions as they sail
above and below the world's oceans as prisoners on the fabulous electric submarine of the
deranged Captain Nemo.
  ISBN 1-4027-2533-7
[1. Science fiction. 2. Submarines (Ships)—Fiction. 3. Sea stories.] I. Title: Twenty thousand leagues
under the sea. II. Andreasen, Dan, ill. III. Verne, Jules, 1828–1905. Vingt mille lieues sous les mers.
IV. Title. V. Series.

PZ7.C4703Aae 2006
[Fic]—dc22

                                          2005014966

Distributed in Canada by Sterling Publishing Co., Inc.
c/o Canadian Manda Group, 664 Annette Street
Toronto, Ontario, Canada M6S 2C8
Distributed in the United Kingdom by GMC Distribution Services,
Castle Place, 166 High Street, Lewes, East Sussex, England BN7 1XU

For information about custom editions, special sales, and premium and corporate purchases,
please contact Sterling Special Sales at 800-805-5489 or specialsales@sterlingpublishing.com.

Manufactured in China

Lot#:
16 18 20 19 17 15
05/17

www.sterlingpublishing.com

Design by Renato Stanisic

CONTENTS

PART I

CHAPTER 1

Monster or Man

The year 1866 will always be remembered for a strange event. For months, sailors around the world were reporting an odd sight. Each of them saw something that was faster and bigger than any sea animal. Sometimes it even looked like it was lit up! The object had been seen by too many people to say that it wasn't real. The mystery did indeed exist.

In April of 1867, a large ship was hit by the beast. The accident scared everyone. Finally people wanted to find this monster who ruled the seas.

It was at this time that I first heard about it. I had spent the last six months doing research in the United States. I was studying the ocean and sea life. My work was very respected by other scientists. People wanted to hear what I thought about the beast. I could only think of two choices. This thing could be a monster that we had never heard of, or it could be some kind of ship.

I didn't think anyone could have built such a ship without others knowing about it. After learning everything I could about this strange object, I decided that it must be some new sea creature. After all, how do we know what lives deep within the ocean waters? We can only guess. Maybe the appearance of this creature was no more than an accident.

After much thought, I formed an answer. The animal must be a narwhal, or unicorn of the sea. But it would be much bigger than a usual narwhal. No, this one would be ten times that size.

And its horn would be six times stronger. Moving at just twenty miles per hour, the beast would become a monster that could control the waters and anything in them.

Word of the beast spread around the world quickly. It was decided that a large ship should set out in search of the beast. The *Abraham Lincoln* left as soon as possible. But just when we were ready to meet the monster, the monster disappeared. Two months went by without anyone seeing it. The *Abraham Lincoln* returned without news. Finally word came from a steamer leaving San Francisco. The monster had been seen! The *Abraham Lincoln* was to set sail once again. It was just three hours before the boat was ready that I received a letter:

> *To Mr. Aronnax, Professor of the Museum of Paris*
> *Sir: If you would like to join the* Abraham Lincoln
> *on this journey, the Government of the United States*

would be happy to have you. Commander Farragut has a cabin ready for you.

Sincerely yours,
J. B. Hobson
Secretary of Marine

I put down the letter. I now knew that I must hunt down the monster. I forgot how tired I was. I didn't give a thought to my friends or my work. I just wanted to leave and begin my search.

Conseil, my servant, came with me on all my travels. I liked him and he liked me. He never asked where we were going or how long we would stay. Besides this, he was a healthy young man. I could count on him to help me load and lift things.

With Conseil's help, I packed my bags.

Upon arriving at the *Abraham Lincoln*, I met the man in charge of the trip.

"I am Pierre Aronnax," I said. I held out

my hand to shake his. "Are you Commander Farragut?" I asked.

The man bowed and smiled. "Your cabin is ready for you."

I followed him, looking at the ship as we passed each part. It was a good boat in which to begin looking for the creature. The *Abraham Lincoln* could go very quickly. Of course, it would never be as fast as the monster. The rooms on board, including my cabin, would be fine for the next several days.

A crowd of people at the dock sent us off. They cheered and wished us luck in finding the beast. The boat soon reached high speed and we pushed full steam into the dark waters of the Atlantic.

CHAPTER 2

Find the Beast

〜

Captain Farragut was a good sailor. It was as if he and the boat were one spirit. It was clear that either this man would eventually kill the sea monster, or else the monster would kill him. I could see no other choice.

The rest of the men on board felt the same. The narwhal must be stopped. When Captain Farragut offered two thousand dollars to the first man to see it, the sailors became even more excited. The most eager of all was a man named Ned Land. Ned was known as the prince of harpooners. He could throw a spear better than any other man. Ned did not think a whale of such great size could exist. He was the only man on board who felt this way. He had a hard time believing that there was a man-made ship out there, but a narwhal seemed impossible. I tried to change his mind, but he was stubborn. A man-made boat just made more sense than a whale.

The captain and crew searched the waters for three months. But as time passed, everyone got tired. It looked as though the narwhal had gone for good. The sailors couldn't hide their disappointment. They were starting to talk of going home, even though Captain Farragut spoke against it. If he was to keep his crew together, he would have to make some changes quickly.

"Give me three days," the captain said. If the monster did not appear in the next three days, the boat would be turned around. The *Abraham Lincoln* would return home.

This gave the crew some hope. If they didn't find the beast, at least they would be going back to their normal lives. The sailors gathered on the deck again. At least one group of men was watching for a sign at all times.

Two days passed. The men tried everything to draw out the monster. They threw food overboard. Small boats went out from the ship, leaving no area of water unsearched. Men searched day and night, but for nothing.

On the third day, the captain had no choice but to turn around. The narwhal was nowhere in sight. Even Captain Farragut knew it was time to head home. But as the boat turned, so did the sailors' luck. A voice rang out through the silence. It was the voice of Ned Land, the only nonbeliever on the ship. And the words he shouted brought everyone running to see.

Captain Farragut gave the order to stop. The ship slowed to a halt, rocking gently with

the waves. I searched the darkness, wondering how the man had seen anything. My heart beat as if it would break. But Ned was not wrong. We all saw the object he pointed to. It lit up the sea with a strange glow. The shine on the water made an oval shape. We could feel the warmth coming from below the water.

One of the officers tried to explain away the object in scientific terms.

"No!" I replied. "See! See! It moves! It is going forward and backward. It is rushing toward us!"

A loud cry rose from the crowd.

"Silence!" said the captain. "Reverse the engines! We need to go back!"

The orders were followed and the ship moved away from the creature.

But the wild beast raced toward us even faster. We held our breath as we waited for the animal to catch us. I secretly prayed, for the

Abraham Lincoln would never survive an attack by a beast of this size.

Suddenly, the light faded. We felt some relief. But then it came up on the other side, as if the animal had slid under our ship. We expected a crash at any moment. Instead, the huge creature raced away without attacking.

The captain had a look of disbelief on his face.

"Mr. Aronnax," he said to me, "I don't know what to think."

I answered with a question to which I already knew the answer. "You now believe this is an animal of nature?"

"I do indeed," the captain replied. "It seems to be a giant electric narwhal."

"I think nothing less than a torpedo will stop this beast," I added.

"Yes. With this power, it must be the most

terrible creature ever created. We must keep watch carefully."

The sailors spent the night watching the sea for a sign. The light from the monster went out around midnight. Within an hour, a loud whistling began. By morning, the crew was getting mad at the animal. They tried harpooning it and shooting it with a gun. Their efforts didn't seem to hurt the beast at all.

Attacks during the day seemed pointless. The beast rarely appeared above the water. When we did see it, we always seemed to be so far behind. As night came, the waters got rough. The lights that shone around the beast allowed us to close in on it more easily. The captain wanted to bring the beast down. Several shots fired by the crew hit the creature. Ned stood watch with his harpoon. I stood with him at the side, praying we would see the beast. When he saw his first chance, Ned threw the harpoon at the animal. I held on to the railing, trying to fight the waves made by the great animal. The harpoon hit a hard object and sent up a blast of water. The blast knocked several men over and threw me overboard before I even knew what was happening.

CHAPTER 3

Sinking, but Saved

౿

The fall I took was so hard that I can't really remember what happened. At first, I sank into the water about twenty feet. I am a good swimmer, so this didn't scare me. I came right back up to the top. But as I looked around in the darkness, I saw a black object disappearing in the east. Its lights were slowly fading. It was the ship! I was lost.

"Help! Help!" I shouted, swimming toward the *Abraham Lincoln.*

My clothes stuck to me and stopped me from

moving around. I was sinking! I was choking!

"Help!"

This was my last cry. My mouth filled with water. I struggled to stay above the water. Suddenly my clothes were grabbed by a strong hand and I felt myself pulled to the surface. Then, I very clearly heard these words whispered in my ear:

"Master, if you would lean on my shoulder, you would swim much easier."

I grabbed Conseil's arm.

"Is that you?" I asked, unsure of where I was.

"It is," answered Conseil, "and I am waiting for your orders."

"I guess we both fell into the sea?"

"No," replied Conseil. "But since you are my master, I followed you in."

It was hard for me to believe that he had actually jumped in after me. But he was a true friend.

"And the ship?" I asked him.

"The ship?" replied Conseil. "I don't think

that you should count on her for help. As I jumped into the water, I heard the men at the wheel say that the screw and the rudder were broken."

"Broken?"

"Yes, broken by the monster's teeth. It is the only damage done to the *Abraham Lincoln*. But she is gone now. We cannot get her attention."

"Then we are lost," I said to myself.

"Perhaps," said Conseil. "But we still have several hours. We can do a lot in that amount of time."

Conseil's worry-free attitude gave me a little hope. But the heaviness of my clothes around me made me think I could not get very far.

"Would you like me to cut them?" Conseil asked. With my permission, he used a knife to cut my clothing from top to bottom. As I began to swim, they slipped off me easily. I did the same for him and we continued to swim next to each other.

But our situation was still terrible. Perhaps no one had noticed we were missing. We still felt that our best hope was to continue swimming toward the ship. It was now the middle of the night. Perhaps by daylight we would be close enough for them to see us.

The tiredness seemed to hit me all at once. I could swim no more. We saw the ship. It was still about five miles away. We cried into the air, even though we would never be heard.

We listened. It may have only been a whistle in my ear, but it seemed to me a cry answered mine.

"Did you hear?" I murmured.

"Yes! Yes!"

Conseil gave one more frantic call.

This time there was no mistake! A human voice answered ours! Was it a voice of another person left in the middle of the ocean? Was a boat from the ship trying to find us in the darkness?

Conseil cried out one last time. Then he fell back into the water, exhausted.

"What did you see?"

"I saw..." he said, saving his breath.

What had he seen? The monster? But what about the voice? I had hardly heard it. My strength was gone. My fingers were stiff. My mouth relaxed and opened, letting the salt water in. The coldness took over my body. I raised my head for the last time and then I sank.

A hard object hit me at just that moment. I clung to it and felt as if I was being pulled up. I felt myself at the top of the water. It was then that I fainted.

The quick rubbing by Conseil brought me back around. I half opened my eyes.

"Conseil!" I murmured. "What do you need?"

Just then, the light of the moon sank down into the horizon. In the glow of light, I saw a face that was not Conseil's. I knew this face right away.

"Ned!" I cried. "Were you thrown into the sea by the rocking of the ship?"

"Yes, Professor, but I was lucky. I found an island."

"An island?" I said.

"Well, I guess I should say I got my footing on the gigantic narwhal."

"What do you mean?" I asked, very confused.

"I did harpoon the beast, but the weapon did not even pierce the skin. In fact, the harpoon bent."

"Why, Ned, why?" I asked.

"Because, Professor, the beast is made out of sheet iron."

Ned's words put so many thoughts in my brain. I climbed to the top of the object and kicked it. The body was hard, not like the outside of most water animals. But could it be a reptile, like a turtle or an alligator?

No. This was a man-made object. It was smooth and made of steel. It was clear that we were lying on the back of some sort of boat. The boat looked like a huge steel fish.

Just then a bubbling began at the back of the strange object. It began to move. We had only enough time to grab hold of the upper part, which stuck about seven feet out of the water.

"As long as it keeps going straight, we will be fine," Ned said. "But if it decides to dive, we are finished."

The night was long, but daylight finally came. The fog from the morning soon left. I could actually begin to see the deck and railing of the machine.

Ned kicked the steel we were standing on. "Open up, Monster!" he said. It took me only a minute to figure out my friend wanted to be let inside. The boat we were on was slowly sinking.

Luckily for us, the sinking stopped. Suddenly a noise, like the banging of metal, came from inside the boat. One metal square was moved and a man appeared. He let out an odd cry and disappeared. Some minutes later, eight strong men appeared. They waved us down inside the machine. We followed, not knowing what to expect.

CHAPTER 4

Two Strangers

෨

We were in the machine in a matter of seconds. I shivered all over. I had no idea what would happen. At first, we were in total darkness. I couldn't see anything. I felt my feet clinging to the steps of a ladder. Ned and Conseil followed me. At the bottom of the ladder a door opened. It shut with a bang.

We were alone. All was black. I could hardly imagine where we were. It was a good half hour before we got some light. It appeared with two men.

One man was short with strong muscles. He had dark hair and a black mustache. The other man was tall with good looks.

The two strangers spoke to each other in a language I had never heard. I spoke up in French and told them I didn't understand.

When I got no answer, I decided to tell my story just in case they might understand a few words. I told them our names, speaking slowly about each one of us.

The men listened to me. I was sure they didn't understand. I nodded for Ned to try in English. They made no reply to him either. Conseil then tried in German, but we got the same blank stares from the men. In a few minutes they left, leaving us confused and scared.

We talked about our situation for a few minutes. Just then the door opened. A man entered with clothes, coats, and pants made of a material I had never seen. We quickly got out of our wet things. As we dressed, the man set the table in the room and put out three plates.

"What do you think they eat here?" asked Ned. "Turtle liver and shark?"

To our surprise, we were treated as if we were in a nice restaurant. We ate several kinds of fish, some of which I had never tasted before. There were other foods that I enjoyed, even though I couldn't tell if they were vegetable or animal. Each of us cleaned our plates. We saw some writing on each one:

MOBILIS IN MOBILI

N.

The letter N was probably the initial of the boat's captain. We didn't spend time thinking about that. We were tired and full from our meal. Ned and Conseil stretched out on the carpet and were soon asleep. I couldn't relax, though. My thoughts were on all that had happened to us in the last several hours. Finally I allowed myself to rest. I fell into a deep, deep sleep in this strange monster we had found.

CHAPTER 5

The *Nautilus*

ᴄᴏ

We slept for a long time. I was glad for the rest because it let my mind think more clearly. Slowly we began to wonder where we were and why we were in a cell. It didn't take us long to notice the heavy air about us. We were having a hard time breathing! Just as I began to worry about being in this ship, a rush of fresh air charged in through a vent. At the same time, the boat began to move.

We discussed our situation. We decided that it must have been a full twenty-four hours since we had eaten our last meal. We were very hungry. Ned was the only one who really seemed upset. The lack of fresh air and his hunger made him mean and angry. When some men finally appeared at our door, Ned jumped on the first one and held him down. Conseil stopped him before he actually hurt the man.

"Control yourself, Mr. Land! And you, Professor, should really listen to me." The words in French made us stand back in surprise. The captain of the ship was speaking to us. Ned stepped back, letting the first man loose. A few minutes went by before the man in charge spoke again.

"Gentlemen," he said. "I speak your language. I know who you are and what you were doing aboard the *Abraham Lincoln.*"

"But sir," I said. "Who are you? And why are you keeping us here?" My words were calm, but I could feel anger inside me.

"I am a man who was tired of the world the way it was. I have created my own world here—one that I will never leave."

"That is fine for you, sir, but what about us? We are not part of your plan." I tried not to sound angry because I didn't know his plans.

"I know that you have been trying to hunt me down for months," the stranger replied. "For that, I dislike you. But since you are here against your will, I will try to make it comfortable for you. You and your friends may have freedom on my ship, unless of course I see a need to keep you hidden. If that happens, you may be kept locked in your cabins."

Our visible anger didn't change the man's mind.

"You will not regret your time here," the stranger said. "As a man who studies the sea, you will find this land of mine amazing."

I had to agree that this place would be

29

wonderful to explore. I decided not to argue and asked him his name instead.

"You may call me Captain Nemo. To me, you are just the passengers of the *Nautilus*."

Two men entered and nodded for Conseil and Ned to follow them. Captain Nemo took me another way. The walk was short and ended in a beautiful dining hall. I took my place at a table set for breakfast. I saw many different foods. I tasted most of them before the captain spoke again.

"The sea is everything. It covers most of the world. It makes me feel free and safe from all harm."

I could tell he meant it. He walked back and forth, talking about everything from the fish to the depth of the waters. When I sensed he was done, I rose. The captain motioned for me to follow him again.

We came to a library. This room was even

more beautiful than the dining room. Every comfort one needed was there.

"What better place is there to read than at the bottom of the sea? I have twelve thousand books here. Here there is silence and privacy."

I quickly agreed and went right to the shelves. I saw books of science and literature. They were written in many different languages. The books all appeared to have been read before. I figured the captain must love this room, coming here often to escape into stories.

"Thank you for allowing me to take in such a pleasure," I said, barely able to step away from the shelves. I didn't know where to start.

The captain laughed in surprise at the new things I was learning. As much as I knew about the sea, the captain still impressed me. And yet, the greatest wonders were still to come. I followed the gentleman on a tour of the *Nautilus*.

From the bathroom to the kitchen, each room was decorated with excellent taste. And the works to keep the ship moving and running smoothly were beyond anything I could have dreamed. The electricity used to run the entire ship left me wanting more information on the fine vessel on which we sailed.

Captain Nemo filled the next several minutes with details about the ship. As a scientist, I understood how the great monster could both rise above the water and sink so far under. Any other listener would have had trouble understanding, but I followed his words with great interest. I still found it amazing that a ship of this type could be built without any country knowing about it. But it was true. And I honestly believe that no other man in the world would have been able to do so. Captain Nemo had brains, wealth, and control. He actually could change the future for people everywhere. I found this thought both scary and comforting. I knew I would be spending a lot of time with this interesting man.

"Join me on the platform?" the captain asked, heading for the staircase. I climbed up the iron steps and found myself on the upper part of the *Nautilus.* Here the sea was beautiful. The sky was pure and a light breeze rippled the waters. I had never felt more excited in my life!

CHAPTER 6

The Start of an Adventure

⌒∂

The waters remained calm and the skies stayed bright. I could see no land on any side. I did not know right away where we were resting. A crewman stepped onto the deck and measured the height of the sun. It was only a matter of seconds until we knew the time of day and our location.

"I now leave you to your studies," Captain Nemo said. "There are maps below for you to follow and room for you to think. I will be in my cabin."

I was surprised at the short amount of time

the captain had spent with me. And yet, I looked forward to the hours on my own. I spent time on the deck and then went to the saloon below. Here there were many maps waiting for me. For a full hour I did nothing but think. I could hardly believe this adventure was true. But the entrance of my two friends made it all seem real.

"Where are we?" asked Ned.

"My friends," I answered, "you are on board the *Nautilus*. We should consider ourselves lucky. This is an amazing ship."

"Lucky!" Ned said loudly. "We are stuck here on a ship of nothing more than iron bars! How could this possibly be lucky?"

I spent the next few minutes trying to impress the man with the things I had seen. I knew Ned couldn't possibly feel as I did. I had seen the beauty and wonder firsthand. And yet, I felt my stories were getting through to him, at least a little bit.

Suddenly, darkness fell upon us. I didn't feel the worry that I had when this happened before. Instead, I waited. I expected to see something wonderful when the light came back. I wasn't disappointed. For the next two hours we were entertained by a show of color and grace. Fish and other creatures I had never seen before swam beside our ship. There were snakes six feet long. Japanese salamanders were everywhere. We couldn't believe the nature surrounding us.

I was so happy to see and study these animals in their own homes. The glow of the ship drew in the fish. I expected to see Captain Nemo again, but he didn't come back. After some time, Ned and Conseil returned to their cabin. I went to my chamber to eat dinner. My meal was made up of turtle soup and a kind of fish that I did not recognize. I spent the rest of the evening reading, writing, and thinking. As the *Nautilus* sped quickly through the Black River, I stretched myself out on the couch and fell asleep.

The next day was the 9th of November. I awoke after a long sleep of twelve hours. I dressed quickly and went to the library. I studied everything I could get my hands on that day. Time moved quickly. The entire day passed without a visit from Captain Nemo. The next day was the same. I did not see one of the ship's crew. Ned and Conseil spent the day with me. They were as surprised as I was that the captain had not visited. Was he sick? Was he too busy to see us?

We were being fed well and were free to roam the ship. I decided that the captain had not forgotten us. The next day I was glad for a change. I could tell by the fresh air spreading through the ship that we had come to the surface of the ocean.

I found the staircase and climbed to the platform. It was six o'clock. The weather was cloudy, but the gray sea was calm. The sun made the fog disappear. I was admiring the sunrise when I heard steps coming up to the platform. I was ready to greet Captain Nemo. Instead, I saw his assistant. He looked at the sea, said a few words in German, and then left. Five days went on like this. Every morning I went to the platform. Every day his assistant went through the same routine. Captain Nemo did not appear.

I had made up my mind that I would never see the man again. But when I returned to my room on the 16th of November, I found a note on the table. It was written in clear, dark print. The letter simply said—

To Professor Aronnax on board the Nautilus:

Captain Nemo invites Professor Aronnax to a hunting-party tomorrow morning. We will visit the forests of the island of Crespo. He hopes nothing will stop the professor from coming. He would be pleased to see him joined by his friends.

Captain Nemo, commander of the Nautilus.

"A hunt!" exclaimed Ned.

"And in the forests of the island of Crespo!" added Conseil.

"Let us first see where the island of Crespo is," I said. I did not share their excitement.

We decided from our map that Crespo is a small island in the middle of the North Pacific. We went to dinner and bed wondering what awaited us.

On waking up the next morning, the 17th of November, I could tell the *Nautilus* was perfectly still. I dressed quickly and entered the library.

Captain Nemo was waiting there for me. He rose, bowed, and asked me if I was ready for my trip.

We entered the dining room, where breakfast was served. Captain Nemo again spoke about the workings of the ship. Today, he told me about the challenges of getting oxygen into the boat. I listened with interest to his knowledge of the sea and the workings of this submarine.

After more talk of air and of the types of hunting guns that would work beneath the sea, Captain Nemo led me down the hall. I called to my two friends as I passed their cabin. They followed right behind us—not knowing what they were in for.

CHAPTER 7

The Walk

The clothes we were to change into were heavy. They were made of rubber with thick boots and gloves. Captain Nemo and one of his men, along with Conseil and I, were soon ready. In the end, Ned had chosen not to go. The poor man felt odd about the whole idea of this trip. And the suit of rubber was enough to make him back out altogether. Perhaps he needed a rest from all this mystery. Maybe, for once, he wanted to sit back and allow someone else to seek out the answers.

For whatever the reason, we gladly left Ned behind and set off without him.

One of the *Nautilus'* crew members handed me a gun made for underwater use. I took it and prepared to put on my helmet. The upper part of our outfit had three holes protected by thick glass. This would let us see in all directions. When the parts on our backs were hooked up, I could breathe in my helmet.

With a lamp hanging from my belt and the gun in my hand, I was ready to set out on my walk. However, I found it impossible to take a step in this suit! I didn't need to worry, though. I felt myself being pushed into a little room. Conseil followed me and a door closed us in. We were once again in darkness.

After a few minutes, we heard a loud hissing. I felt the cold water rising around me. A second door opened. We saw a faint light. In another moment our feet were on the bottom of the sea.

How can I even begin to explain how great that walk under the water was? I no longer felt the weight of my clothing, my shoes, my air supply, or my thick helmet.

The light around me was unbelievable! The sun's rays shone easily through the water. I could clearly make out objects that were a hundred and fifty yards away.

I stomped through the sand for a quarter of an hour. What a feast for the eyes! I saw flowers, bits of rock, plants, shells, and sea life. It was amazing! All of these wonders I saw in just a quarter of a mile! Captain Nemo waved me on. I continued. The sand beneath us turned to a slimy mud. Next we traveled over a carpet of seaweed. With each step, I learned more and more about this world under the sea. I wished I were taking notes. I had so many things to say! The sun, now hitting the water in a different way, made everything look different. I looked at the fish and the weeds through which they seemed to enjoy swimming. Just as I became very interested, Captain Nemo stopped. He waited until I joined him, then pointed to a huge object in the shadows, a short bit away.

"It is the forest of the island of Crespo," I thought. I was not mistaken.

We had at last arrived on the borders of this forest. The woods were made up of large tree-plants. This place was perfect. Neither the stems nor branches of any plants were broken or bent. Everything stood straight and tall. Science could explain why these plants grew the way they did, but I didn't take the time to think it through. I was spending my time getting used to the darkness around us. I explored for about an hour before Captain Nemo gave the sign to stop. I was glad for a break. I lay down on the straight grass. This short rest relaxed me.

After four more hours of walking I needed a

nap. My eyes soon closed behind the thick glasses and I fell into a heavy sleep. Captain Nemo did the same.

How long I slept, I'm not sure. When I woke up, the sun seemed to be setting. Captain Nemo had already gotten up. I began to stretch my arms when something brought me quickly to my feet.

A huge sea-spider with squinting eyes was watching me from a few steps away. It looked ready to spring on me! I shuddered with horror, even though I knew the suit would protect me. It was only a matter of seconds before the ugly creature died. Captain Nemo had used his gun. It made me realize that as beautiful as this world was, it could still be a very dangerous place.

Again we walked. The ground was on somewhat of a hill. I noticed the area getting darker and there were walls around us. The sun would not reach here, so it became very hard to see. I was feeling my way along when suddenly I saw a

brilliant white light. Captain Nemo had just put on his electric lamp. Conseil and I did the same.

Captain Nemo was still pushing his way into the dark depths of the forest. I saw that the plant life was slowly disappearing. As we walked, I had the feeling that eyes were on me. I believed there were sea creatures hiding in the dark. I even saw Captain Nemo raise his gun at one point, wait, and then move on carefully. After many hours our walk began to slow down. I looked ahead to see a wall of rocks before us. It took me a moment to understand. This was the island of Crespo. Captain Nemo stopped suddenly. A wave of his hand made us all stop as well. As much as I wanted to climb over that wall, I knew this was the end.

The return began. We took a different path back to the ship. This road was very steep and painful. But the light of the sun soon returned and I felt a little more refreshed. I noticed the return of the fish and other sea creatures right away. At one point I saw the captain shoot into some shrubs near the surface of the water. I heard a soft hissing and a creature fell before us. It was a sea-otter. It was five feet long and looked like the type of animal whose fur would have been made into a coat in most countries. Captain Nemo's companion took the beast and threw it over his shoulder. We continued on our journey.

I would be glad to get back. The air I was supplied with seemed to be getting thin. I was walking along when I saw Captain Nemo coming quickly toward me. He bent me to the ground. The captain's companion did the same thing to Conseil. I watched as Captain Nemo lay down beside me and stayed very still.

My body froze as I looked up to see two sharks. I knew from my research that these were tintoreas—terrible creatures that could crush a whole man in their jaws.

Luckily these sharp-teethed creatures do not see very well. They passed without seeing us. I was so happy when we reached the *Nautilus*. All I wanted was to go to my cabin for food and sleep. I knew my dreams would be of our adventure at the bottom of the sea.

CHAPTER 8

A Few Days on Land

By the next morning I had slept off my tiredness from the day before. I spoke with Captain Nemo about the wonders of the waters we had visited. It was so exciting to see the types of fish and sea life that lived at different depths in the water. Each creature had what it needed to stay alive in its sea home. I also asked the scientist about the world's oceans and how deep the different areas were. He knew many from memory. He said the area where we were now, in this part of the Pacific, was about four thousand yards deep.

"If you took all the oceans in the world and averaged their depths to make a flat sea bottom, the depth would be about one and three-quarter leagues, or roughly five miles." The captain's words added to the research I was doing and answered some questions of my own that I really had been wondering about.

I saw very little of Captain Nemo over the next month. I guess we were both busy with our studies and the duties of everyday life. December came upon us quickly. I had been studying the islands as we met them. To the average person, they were just chunks of land surrounded by water on all sides. To me, they were great reefs or deposits made from volcanoes or nearby mountains. I watched the walls closely as we passed them each day, using the electric light we had to show them brightly. I learned as much as I could when chances came.

Weeks passed. We came upon sunken ships,

schools of fish more colorful than I ever imagined, and rough waters that rocked the *Nautilus*. One day a sudden shock hit our vessel. The *Nautilus* had just touched a rock, but it was enough to make it stuck. I could have seen this as a problem, but instead I saw it as a chance. Ned agreed with me.

"That is an island. On that island there are trees. Under those trees are animals. We can make them into roast beef and cutlets."

"Will the captain let us visit this land?" Conseil asked.

I was curious, too, about what Captain Nemo would say. I asked him and he gave in easily. At eight o'clock, armed with guns and axes, my two friends and I got off the *Nautilus*.

Being on land again felt wonderful! I took in the surroundings like I took in breaths of air. The greatness of the trees struck me first. The generous plants gave us nuts, which in turn gave us milk to drink and nuts to eat. Our walks through the forest brought many wonders. We found pigeons to eat, but these just made us wish for more. The wild hogs and bouncing rabbit kangaroos we found filled our stomachs with what we had been dreaming of—real meat. The fish on board the *Nautilus* was delicious, but we all longed for that taste of meat, which was like no other. We enjoyed our time off the ship, relaxing and studying this world around us. If it hadn't been for the natives following us, it would have been a perfect trip.

Captain Nemo told us that even when all the natives of Papua were together on shore, we would have nothing to fear. By the next morning, though, there were at least five or six hundred of the people around. They were strong-looking people. Their simple clothing was well suited to the climate. Some of the women had herbs and vegetables around their waists. Almost all of them had bows, arrows, and shields on their shoulders.

I talked to Captain Nemo about them. I told him the fears I had. "We need to open our hatches tomorrow to renew the air of the *Nautilus*. They will surely jump out of their canoes and climb aboard."

"Well, then, let them come in," the captain answered. "Tomorrow at twenty minutes to three P.M., the tide will push us off this rock and we will once again be on our way."

I slept soundly. I woke at six the next morning. The hatches had not yet been opened. We still had air in storage but we were running dangerously low. At twenty-five minutes to three, Captain Nemo appeared in the saloon.

"We are going to start," he said. "I have given the orders to open the hatches."

"And the Papuans? Won't they leap over the hatches you have opened" I asked.

"Come and you will see."

Ned and Conseil were watching the ship's crew around the hatches. Cries of fear and rage were heard from outside. Horrible faces met us when we looked outside. The natives were turning back, yelling as loudly as when they had come. Only this time, it was because they were in pain.

The natives had not touched a rail when they tried to come on board. They had touched a metal cable or wire, one that Captain Nemo had charged with electricity. Whoever touched it felt a powerful shock. The shock was not strong enough to kill anyone, but it did scare them. It was enough to make them turn back and allow us to leave.

With the natives gone and the *Nautilus* free once again, the ship swept through the waters slowly. We were off for more adventure.

CHAPTER 9

A Safe Resting Place

ᴄᴏ

It was now the middle of January. We were headed for the Indian Ocean. The *Nautilus* was moving quickly and smoothly. I wondered where the great Captain Nemo would take us next. I knew he was studying water temperatures right now. This wonderful vessel allowed him to experiment like no other scientist had before. He could find water samples at depths no other man could reach.

On one particular morning, the weather was stormy, causing the sea to be rough and rolling.

There was a strong east wind. I went up on the platform to see the horizon. As I did so, I met up with Captain Nemo.

For some minutes he didn't move. He was looking through a glass telescope at something in the distance. He put down his telescope and walked to the other side of the platform. He didn't even see me. He kept stopping to watch the sea. I couldn't guess what he was thinking of. The *Nautilus* was hundreds of miles from the nearest land.

I decided to look on my own. I went to the drawing room and took out a telescope that I used regularly. I had no sooner set my eye to peer through it than it was quickly taken out of my hands.

I turned around. Captain Nemo was before me, but I barely recognized him. His face was so different. His eyes flashed with fire. His teeth were set and his body was stiff. He clenched his fists and puffed out his chest. He didn't move. My glass, which had fallen from his hands, rolled around at his feet.

What had I done to make him so angry? No, I wasn't the reason for his mood. His eyes were still fixed on the horizon. He spoke, his words making little sense.

"You must do what we agreed upon," he said.

I looked at him strangely, letting him know I didn't understand any of this.

"You and your companions must stay in your cabins until I tell you otherwise." His words were strong. He wasn't in the mood for arguing.

"You are the master," I replied. "But may I ask you a question?"

"No," he said.

I walked away, knowing it was useless to argue. My friends were as confused as I was. We waited in silence in a cabin. Instead of answers, though, we got breakfast. We ate. Just then, the lamp that lit the room went out and left us in total darkness. Ned and Conseil were soon asleep. In spite of my best try, I also closed my eyes and drifted off. Something must have been put in our food to make us sleepy.

The next day I woke with my thoughts clear. The ship sailed on as if nothing had happened. Maybe nothing had.

I met up with the captain at about two o'clock. I was in the drawing room sorting my notes when he opened the door.

"Are you a doctor?" he asked, taking me by surprise.

"I am," I said. "I worked as a doctor and a surgeon for several years."

"Mr. Aronnax, will you take a look at one of my men?" The captain looked worried.

"Is he sick?" I asked.

"Yes. Follow me."

I followed the captain onto the deck and to a cabin in the sailors' section of the boat. On a bed there lay a man about forty years of age. He was not only sick, he was hurt. His head was covered in loose bandages. I undid the wrapping. It was a horrible wound. I had no doubt that the man was going to die.

"What caused the wound?" I asked, trying to imagine what force had done this type of damage to the sailor.

Captain Nemo ignored my question. "How is he?"

I sighed, then took the captain aside. "He will be dead within two hours."

"But what can you do to save him?" the captain asked, his eyes begging now for help.

I hated to give him my answer. "There is nothing, sir. Nothing."

I watched as Captain Nemo's eyes filled with

tears. I didn't think he was capable of feeling sorrow.

The captain's hands touched the man gently and some tears appeared in his eyes. For some moments I stayed to watch the dying man. The sick man lay still, but the captain was the one who most interested me. He would go from near tears to a hardness that reminded me that grown men usually don't cry. Several times I saw him grow uncomfortable because I was still there. Finally I think he realized that I would be of no help.

"You may leave now, Mr. Aronnax," said the captain.

I left the two alone, feeling sorry for both of them. The dying sailor haunted my thoughts for the rest of the night.

The next morning I went to the bridge. Captain Nemo was there before me. As soon as he saw me, he came over to me.

"Professor, would you like to take a walk today?"

"With my friends?" I asked.

"If they like."

We were ready within a half an hour. Captain Nemo and half a dozen crew members left with us. The boat rested on the bottom of the sea. We walked along the floor for at least two hours, looking at the coral and the beauty of the plant life. We were on a carpet of flowers with gems of beauty surrounding us everywhere.

Captain Nemo stopped. My friends and I stopped as well and turned around. I saw the crew members form a semicircle around their chief. I then watched as four of the men brought forth a long object of rectangular shape.

With a sign from Captain Nemo, one of the men stepped ahead and began to dig a hole with a pickax that he took from his belt. I then understood it all. This was a cemetery! This was for the man who had died in the night! The captain and his men had come to bury their companion in this general resting place at the bottom of the ocean.

I watched as the man was buried and honored at his grave. When we got back to the ship, I approached Captain Nemo about the ceremony.

"He rests now, near his friends, in the coral cemetery?"

"Yes," the captain replied. "Forgotten by all else, but not by us."

"Your dead sleep quietly, Captain. At least they are out of the reach of sharks."

"Yes, sir," the captain replied gravely. "Of sharks and *men*."

PART II

CHAPTER 10

A Sea of Treasures

⌒

We now come to the second part of the journey under the sea. The first ended with the moving scene in the coral cemetery. On the 24th day of January, 1868, I mounted the platform and watched an officer measure the height of the sun.

We were exploring the waters of the Indian Ocean. An average person would have been bored on this trip. The hours would have seemed too long. But the daily walks on the platform, the sight of the rich waters, the books in the library, and the daily log of sights were heaven to me. It took up all my time and left not a moment for weariness.

For the next few weeks, the sea life and birds along the surface of the ocean pleased me. Captain Nemo saw my excitement and offered me an invitation.

"That is the island of Ceylon, famous for its pearl-fisheries. Would you like to visit one of them, Mr. Aronnax?"

"Certainly, Captain."

"By the way, you are not afraid of sharks?" he asked.

"Sharks!" I exclaimed.

"Yes, you know the fish . . . are you afraid of them?"

"Well, Captain, I am not very familiar with them," I said, being truthful.

"*We* are used to them," the captain said. "In time you will be, too. However, we will be armed. We may even want to hunt the species. So until tomorrow, sir. And be ready to leave early."

Captain Nemo left me with that thought. I allowed the threat of sharks to scare me. Surely the good captain would never put us in any position where we would be in danger. Would he?

Ned and Conseil entered within a few minutes. They already knew about the visit tomorrow and seemed rather excited. I thought they were very brave not even to mention the sharks.

"Before we go, I would like to ask about the pearl," Ned said. "What exactly is a pearl?"

I found it strange that Ned would ask about a pearl before a shark, but I answered him anyway.

"A pearl is what grows inside an oyster," I began. I went on, telling him the details, many of which I didn't think he cared to know. Thinking that he wasn't going to bring up the subject of sharks, I decided to do so myself.

"By and by," I said, trying to take Captain

Nemo's careless tone. "Are you afraid of sharks, brave Ned?"

"Of course not," he answered. "My job in life is as a harpooner."

"But this is quite different, my friend," I said. I was trying to make him see the difference in the two situations. "One might happen along when you are not looking for him. What then?"

"I will deal with it then." Ned laughed, shaking off the question. I could tell I wouldn't get his concern. I decided it was best to keep my fears to myself.

The next morning at four o'clock, we were off to find the pearls. The group of us left in a boat, rowing our way to the area of the pearl-fisheries.

"In a month, this area will be filled with fishing boats. The divers' finds will be well worth their time and work." Captain Nemo spoke from experience.

We put on our rubber clothes and prepared to go where the eager divers would. During our walk, we saw the sea's treasures. The pearls were beautiful! I was amazed by their number and their size. As we walked, we came upon an Indian fisherman. He was most likely a poor man who needed to use his time searching for any pearls he could find. The diver did not see us. We watched with interest when, suddenly, the Indian was on the ground. He made a wave of terror with his right hand and tried get back to the top of the water. I understood his fear. A shark of enormous size was coming at him. The beast's eyes were on fire and his jaws were open. The horror left me unable to move.

The shark twisted, ready to attack the Indian. I saw Captain Nemo rise suddenly, prepare his knife, and walk straight to the monster. The very second the shark was going to snap the fisherman in two, it noticed its new enemy.

The fight began.
The captain thrust
his knife into the shark's side. I could
tell it felt pain, but the shark was a huge animal.
One wound would not take it down. The two
fought one another. I could see Captain Nemo
wearing down, his battle against such a large animal too difficult even for him. The captain fell to
the floor. The shark's jaws opened wide. It should
have been all over for the sea lover. Instead, harpoon in hand, Ned rushed toward the shark and
struck it with a sharp point. The fight was over.

We spent the next few minutes trying to bring
the Indian around. Happily, the man began to
wake up. He opened his eyes. The terror on his
face grew at seeing four men leaning over him.
He sat up, still confused by what had happened.

When the captain knew that the man had his
senses about him again, he pulled from his pocket
a bag of pearls and placed it in the man's hand.

This small treasure, a gift from a man of the waters to the poor fisherman, was accepted with a trembling hand. The man's wondering eyes showed that he didn't know to what beings he owed both his money and his life.

The boat flew over the waves on the way back. Some minutes after we left, we met the shark's dead body floating. We had indeed all been lucky to escape with our lives.

There were two important things I came away knowing that evening. The first was that Captain Nemo was a brave person. The second was that the good captain really did care for members of the human race. This man was full of surprises.

CHAPTER 11

A Plan for Escape

c✧

Over the next month, our travels took us many places. By the middle of February, the *Nautilus* rose to the surface of the Mediterranean.

Upon hearing of our location, Ned took me aside for a talk.

"What I have to tell you is very simple," he said. "I want to leave the *Nautilus*."

I did not wish to keep my friends from being free, but I was not ready to leave the ship. I was learning too much from my journey and from the great Captain Nemo. Each day I got closer to finishing my studies. And would I ever again have a chance like this to observe the wonders of the world? No, certainly not!

"Ned, my friend," I said. "Answer me truthfully. Are you tired of being on board? Are you sorry that you ever met Captain Nemo?"

It took Ned a few minutes before he could answer. "Well," he began, "I don't hate it that I was on this journey under the seas. I will have been glad I made it. But now that we have been here awhile, I want to be finished."

"It will come to an end, Ned."

"Where and when?"

"I don't know," I said. "Perhaps in six months?"

"And where shall we be in six months?"

"Perhaps China? You know the *Nautilus* is a fast traveler."

Ned seemed to think about this for a moment.

"Sir," he said, his face deep in thought, "if Captain Nemo gave you your freedom today, would you take it?"

"I don't know," I answered.

"And," he continued, "what if the question was for today only. What if he would never ask it again?"

"Ned, my friend, I cannot answer that now. I do know, however, that one thing is clear: Captain Nemo captured us. He brought us along with the idea that we will be here as long as he is. If we were to make a plan to leave, it would have to be an escape plan. He could not find out."

"I agree," Ned said, sounding hopeful.

"If, or when, we leave, we must make it during our first try. If we fail, we will never find another time. Captain Nemo will see to that. The captain will never forgive us either."

"So if the time comes when we think we may have a good chance to run, we should take it? No matter if it is two days from now or two months from now?" Ned asked.

"Yes. Now Ned, will you please tell me what a 'good chance to run' is?" I waited for my companion's answer.

"It will be on a dark night. The *Nautilus* should be only a short distance from the coast of Europe."

"And are we to save ourselves by swimming to this coast?" I asked, fearing the answer.

"Yes," Ned said. "If we are close enough to the bank and if the ship is floating at that time. But if the land is far away and the boat is under the water..."

"Then what?" I asked.

"In that case," Ned answered, "I would have to take over the ship. I know how it works. I could get to the controls, draw the bolts, and come to the surface of the water without the captain even knowing our plan."

I listened carefully to his idea.

"Watch for the chance to run, my friend, but remember. One mistake will ruin us."

"I will not forget, sir," Ned answered.

"And now, Ned, would you like to know what I think of your project?"

"Certainly, Mr. Aronnax."

"I think this chance will never come for us."

"Why not?"

"Because Captain Nemo knows we haven't given up our hope for freedom. He will be watching us, especially when we are so close to the European coast."

"We shall see," said Ned, shaking his head.

"Ned," I added, "let us stop here. Do not say another word on the subject. When the right day comes, let us know. We will follow you. I trust you entirely."

Thus ended our conversation.

CHAPTER 12

Strange Happenings

⌒∽

The waters we traveled in were so different that it always seemed there was something new and amazing to study. One night I was in the saloon studying the fish of Archipelago. Captain Nemo entered the room. He didn't notice me there. He seemed to be in his own little world. I allowed him his mood and went about watching the gobies that the ship had just come upon. These little fish made for great study and enjoyment.

In the middle of my work, a man appeared in the waters. He was a diver. He carried a leather purse on his belt. At first I had thought it might be a body of a lost sailor. Maybe a poor soul fallen overboard, or a victim of sharks. But it was a living man. He was swimming strongly, disappearing now and then to the surface for a breath.

I turned toward Captain Nemo and yelled, "A man shipwrecked! We have to save him!"

The captain did not answer me, but came and leaned against the window. The man had reached the ship and had flattened his face against the glass. He was looking in at us.

To my great amazement, Captain Nemo signed to him. The diver answered him with his hand, swam right to the surface of the water, and did not appear again.

"Don't worry about him," said Captain Nemo. "That is Pesca. He is a bold diver. He is very used to the water. Pesca lives more in the sea than on land. He is always going from one island to another."

The captain again ignored my presence and walked past me to a chest with iron locks. On the cover was a copper plate. Inside were bars and bars of gold. My mind wandered. Where did he get this gold? How much was it worth? What was he going to do with it?

I didn't say a word. I watched as Captain Nemo took the bars one by one and arranged them in the chest. I guessed there had to be at least four thousand pounds of gold there.

The captain locked the chest and wrote an address on the lid. With this done, he pressed a button that called for four men to appear. It took all their might to push the chest out of the saloon. At that moment, Captain Nemo turned to me.

"And you were saying, sir?" he said.

"I didn't say anything, Captain."

"Then, sir, I will wish you good night."

The captain turned and left the saloon.

I returned to my room to think. I couldn't sleep. Not after what I had just seen. I was lying in bed when I felt the ship rise to the surface. I could hear a small boat as it set out across the waves. Two hours later, I heard the same noise again. The boat came back and the submarine again sank deep into the waters. So, those millions had been delivered.

The next day I talked to Ned and Conseil about the gold. They were surprised, just as I was. We came up with no possible answer.

I returned to the saloon and worked until five o'clock in the evening going over my notes. By the end of the day, I felt the ship growing hot. This seemed very strange. It soon got so hot, in fact, that I thought there may be a fire on board.

I was leaving the saloon when Captain Nemo entered. He walked toward the thermometer, looked at it, and then turned to me.

I spoke before he could. "If it gets much hotter, we won't be able to stand it."

"Oh," the captain said, "it won't get hotter if we don't want it to."

"You can lower the heat?" I asked eagerly.

"No," he said. "But we can go farther away from where it started. You see, we are floating in a stream of boiling water."

"Is that possible?" I exclaimed.

"Look!"

The panels around the windows opened and I saw the sea totally white in color. A light smoke was curling around the waves, which boiled like water on a stove. I put my hands on one of the windows. It was so hot that I quickly took it off again.

"This is the volcanic part of the seas," Captain Nemo explained. "These are strange happenings. The islands sink under the waves only to rise again later."

By this time, the sea, which till now had been white, was red. I was choking. I was gasping for air.

The captain gave an order. The *Nautilus* left the heat. Fifteen minutes later, we were breathing fresh air on the surface of the ocean. As I looked out upon the waves, a thought struck me. If Ned had chosen this part of the sea for our escape, we would never have made it out alive.

CHAPTER 13

The Escape

⌒

By the end of February, the *Nautilus* was moving through the water of the Atlantic Ocean at a smooth pace. We had traveled nearly ten thousand leagues in three and a half months. That distance is greater than the huge circle of the earth! But where were we going now? We had just finished our tour of the Mediterranean. It was an amazing body of water to study. Now we had returned to the surface of the waves, giving us once again the joy of daily walks on the platform.

Ned was upset that we never had the chance

to escape from the ship. Freedom was always the first thing on his mind.

"I know you are upset, my friend, that you never got to put your plan into action. But to have tried to leave the *Nautilus* in that heat would have killed us all."

Ned did not answer. He had a frown on his face.

"Let's wait and see," I said. "Don't give up hope yet. We will be near France and England in the weeks to come. We could easily find help there."

Ned stared at me. "We will leave tonight."

I gasped at his words. I was not ready for what he said. I tried to answer, but words would not even form in my mouth.

"We agreed to wait for the right time," continued Ned, "and the time has come. Tonight we will be only a few miles from the Spanish coast. It is cloudy. The wind blows freely. You promised me and I am counting on you."

I stayed silent, still not knowing what to say.

"Tonight, at nine o'clock," he said. "I have already told Conseil. Captain Nemo will be in his room by then. The ship's crew will not be able to see us. Conseil and I will take the main stairs. You should wait in the library for our signal. The boat is ready for us. Everything is set for tonight."

"The sea is bad."

"That may be," Ned said, "but we must risk that. We want our freedom! Besides, the boat is strong. And a few miles with a fair wind to carry us is no big deal. So, I bid you good-bye until tonight."

With these words, the man left me. I sat there, wondering how this could be possible. I could run to Captain Nemo and tell him of the plan. But then I would be changing the future for my friends. They did so badly want their freedom. I was confused. I could feel the ship sinking under the waves of the Atlantic as I sorted my thoughts.

I couldn't decide between getting my freedom and leaving the *Nautilus*.

What awful hours passed! Sometimes I would picture my friends and myself safely landed with our freedom. Other times I would imagine something happening to prevent us from leaving. Rather than feeling disappointment like my friends, I would feel joy.

Twice I went to the saloon. I wanted to check the compass. I wanted to see if the *Nautilus* was heading closer to or moving farther away from the coast. The ship was on course to make Ned's plan work. I didn't really have to prepare to leave. My notes were the only things I owned.

I began to think about Captain Nemo. How would he feel about our escape? I had no reason to feel bad for him. After all, he had kept us here against our will. And yet, I wondered if it would upset him.

I hadn't seen the captain for many days.

Would I have the chance to see him before we left? I hoped for it and against it at the same time. I waited. It was the longest day I could remember. My patience was running out.

My dinner was served in my room as usual. I didn't eat much. I wasn't hungry. I left the table at about seven o'clock. I was one hundred and twenty minutes away from the moment when I would join my friends to leave. My heart beat wildly. I was growing more scared by the minute.

I wanted to see the saloon for the last time. I went downstairs to the museum where I had spent so many happy hours. I looked at all its riches, all its treasures. It was hard for a man like me to leave this all behind.

In passing through the saloon, I came near the door to the captain's room. To my great surprise, the door was open. I quickly leaned back. If the captain was in his room, he could see me. But hearing no noise, I went closer. The room was empty. I pushed open the door and took some steps forward.

Suddenly the clock struck eight. My eyes fell upon the compass. We were still traveling north. Our speed was normal and we were at a depth of about sixty feet.

I returned to my room and dressed warmly. I put on sea boots, an otter skin cap, and a coat lined with sealskin. I was ready and waiting.

At a few minutes to nine, I put my ear to the

captain's door. I heard no noise. I returned to the saloon, which was empty.

I opened the door connecting to the library. All was quiet there, too. I stood by the door leading to the main staircase and waited for Ned's signal.

At that moment, the movement of the vessel stopped. That meant we were resting on the bottom of the ocean. I grew more worried. I wished that I could find Ned and tell him to put off this escape.

The door of the saloon opened and Captain Nemo appeared. He saw me and said, "Ah, sir! I have been looking for you. Do you know the history of Spain?"

My nerves wouldn't let me answer.

"Did you hear my question?" Captain Nemo asked again. "Do you know the history of Spain?"

"Not well," I said.

"Well, sit down and I will tell you a strange story," Captain Nemo began.

I listened as the captain started his story. It began back in 1702. I knew most of the history he was telling me, but I still didn't understand why I should be interested.

"So, on October 22nd, 1702, the English ships arrived in Vigo Bay. Admiral Chateau-Renaud fought bravely, but he knew the riches he had would fall into the enemy's hands. So he burned all the treasure ships, which went to the bottom of the ocean."

At this, the captain stood and told me to follow him. The saloon was dark but the waves were sparkling outside the glass windows. I looked.

For half a mile around the *Nautilus*, the waters seemed to glow. The sandy bottom was clean and bright. Some crew members were clearing away broken cases to get to the treasures. And the treasures they found were more beautiful than words. There were trunks of gold and silver, and mounds of jewelry. The sand was piled high with it. The men picked up what they could. They carried it to the ship, placed it inside the vessel, and then went out for more.

I understood now. This was the scene of the battle of October 22nd, 1702. On this very spot, the ships filled with treasures for the Spanish government had sunk. It was now Captain Nemo's hiding spot. His bank was a place safer than anywhere else on earth to keep one's treasures.

"Did you know the sea held such precious gems?" the captain asked with a smile.

"I did," I replied. "But I didn't know the amount and I certainly didn't know where."

"For any country to come take this wealth from the ocean bottom would be silly. They would spend more money trying to get it than they would end up with. But I can take these treasures easily. I have found them not only in Vigo Bay, but in a thousand other spots where shipwrecks have happened." Captain Nemo seemed quite pleased with himself.

"But what about the men who try this adventure on their own for nothing? Think of the money they will be out, not knowing you have already taken these treasures! Is this truly fair to them?"

I had no sooner said these words than I knew they had hurt the captain.

"Do you think that it is not fair that I have these riches? How do you know that *I* do not make good use of them? Do you think that I really don't know there are people out there who are cold and hungry?"

Captain Nemo stopped speaking after that last sentence. He probably felt bad that he had said so much. But I guessed that whatever made him want to share this wealth left him a man whose heart still beat for the suffering of people. I now understood who the riches were meant for when the *Nautilus* had been sailing in the waters of Crete. As we sailed around the world, the mighty captain gave these treasures to the poor and hungry. He helped those in need everywhere. The man whom I believed to hate mankind was really one of the most caring men of all. The good captain's heart was a treasure as well.

I turned down the captain's offer to go out with the crewmen. Instead, I watched from the windows as the men worked with more riches than I ever imagined possible. A warm feeling spread over me as I imagined the people who were helped by these treasures of the sea.

CHAPTER 14

A Walk in the Rain

∽

The next morning, the 19th of February, Ned entered my room. I expected this visit. He looked very disappointed.

"Well, sir?" he said.

"Well, Ned. We lost the chance again," I said. I tried to act disappointed for his sake.

"Yes," Ned said. "That captain decided to stop at exactly the time we planned on leaving his ship."

"I know. He had business at his banker's."

"His banker's!" Ned exclaimed.

"Well, I guess I could say his 'special spot.' By that I mean the ocean bed. His riches are safer there than in chests on land."

I then told Ned about last night. I was hoping he would change his mind about leaving the ship. Instead, he just showed disappointment that he had not been able to take a walk on the battlefield of Vigo himself.

"Well, never mind about last night," Ned said. "We still have tonight."

"What direction is the *Nautilus* going?" I asked.

"I don't know," replied Ned. "We'll find out at noon."

Ned returned to Conseil. I dressed and went to the saloon. The direction on the compass wouldn't please Ned. We were turning our backs on Europe.

For myself, I was not really sorry. I was able to return to my work with some level of calmness.

That night at about eleven o'clock, I received

an unexpected visit from Captain Nemo. He asked me if I would like to see the ocean underworld at night.

"I warn you, the way will be tiring. We shall have far to walk. And we will have to climb a mountain. The roads are not well kept."

I didn't have to think long.

"I'm ready!"

We dressed in our diving suits with the help of crew members. I noticed this was a walk for the captain and me alone. I thought briefly about how angry Ned would be that he once again hadn't been invited on an adventure. But I didn't have time to worry over that. In a few moments, we were ready.

"Where are our electric lamps?" I asked.

"They will be useless," the captain replied.

I didn't think I had heard him right but I couldn't question him. The captain's head disappeared into a metal case. With a few more snaps and pulls, the two of us were both walking on the bottom of the Atlantic.

It was almost midnight and the waters were very dark. But the captain pointed out in the distance a reddish spot about two miles from the *Nautilus*. I had no idea what it was or why it was there. I only knew we were heading toward it.

As we walked, I could hear a pattering above my head. It took me a moment to figure out the sound. Rain! It was rain hitting the waves hard in the middle of a storm! I couldn't help but laugh at the odd idea.

We continued on. I noticed the soil becoming stony. The red light in the distance became brighter. I tried to make stories up in my mind for where we were going. I could tell Captain Nemo had traveled this path often. I followed him. I knew he would get us there safely.

It was one in the morning when we arrived at

the first slopes of the mountain. But to get to them, we had to climb over an area of dead trees. These trees, which had no leaves or sap, had toppled over. They were mixed with seaweed and other ocean life, and seemed impossible to pass. I followed my guide, who never seemed to get tired. We climbed rocks and used a stick to jump over cracks and holes.

Two hours after leaving the *Nautilus*, we had crossed the line of trees and saw the top of the mountain a hundred feet above our heads. The signs of ocean life around me made my blood run cold. There were giant lobsters moving their claws toward us. Huge crabs pointed at us like guns. Large antennae blocked our way, making me feel as if I was where I didn't belong.

When we made it through, we were on the first platform. The sights before me were surprising. Everything was man-made instead of natural.

There were huge piles of rocks, shaped like castles and temples. Instead of ivy seaweed, there were vegetable plants. But what was this place? Who put these stones there? Where had Captain Nemo brought me?

We continued on to the top. I looked down the side we had just climbed. My eyes looked over a large lit-up space. In fact, the mountain was a volcano.

This peak was spitting out red-hot lava in a rain of stones and liquid. The area was lit up like a torch. I followed the mass of red with my eyes, watching as it fell below. What I saw made me shake my head. There, destroyed and ruined, lay a town. Its roofs were open to the sky and its temples had fallen. There were sunken walls, empty streets, and ports that had once held ships on the borders of the ocean.

Where was I? I had to know! I tried to speak, but Captain Nemo stopped me with a wave of his

hand. He picked up a piece of chalk stone, walked to a black rock, and traced one word:

ATLANTIS

I couldn't believe what I read! Atlantis, the ancient continent of the Atlantic Ocean. Could it be? This continent was said to have sunken away undersea because of a huge volcano. No one had ever found it. In fact, many people believe it never existed in the first place. But if it did, and maybe it does, I knew Captain Nemo would be the one to find it. Either way, I knew I was looking at a very old city.

I walked through the place, touching ruins a thousand generations old. I tried to fix in my mind every detail of this great landscape. I looked toward Captain Nemo. He was leaning on a mossy stone, standing very still. Was he dreaming of those men long since disappeared? What wouldn't I give to know his thoughts right then?

We stayed in this place for an hour. I memorized the land under the bright lava and the trembling beneath my feet. Even the sound would stay with me forever. I would never forget what the captain had shared with me.

CHAPTER 15

The Coal Mine

~

The next day, the 20th of February, I woke up very late. It was eleven o'clock before I got dressed and headed for the saloon to check the compass for our direction. It said we were heading south at a speed of twenty miles an hour and at a depth of fifty fathoms.

I noticed the species of fish out the windows. I had seen even the rare ones so much that I hardly thought about them anymore. And yet they were of incredible color and spirit. By four o'clock I began to grow tired. I was worn out from the long night before. I went back to my cabin and spent the evening quietly before going to bed.

It was eight o'clock the next day when I entered the saloon. I looked at the instruments. They said the *Nautilus* was floating on the surface of the ocean. I heard footsteps above me. I went to the platform, but instead of broad daylight, I was surrounded by blackness. Was it still night? No, not a star was shining.

I didn't know what to think when a voice near me said:

"Is that you, Professor?"

"Ah! Captain," I answered. "Where are we?"

"Underground, sir."

"Underground!" I exclaimed. "And the *Nautilus* is still floating?"

"It always floats."

"But I don't understand."

"Wait a few minutes. Our lanterns will be lit and you will see."

I stood on the platform and waited. It was so dark that I couldn't even see Captain Nemo. The lantern was lit. I closed my eyes for a second and then looked again. The *Nautilus* was stopped, floating near a mountain. We were in a lake with high walls all around us.

"Where are we?" I asked.

"In an old volcano that stopped working years ago," Captain Nemo replied.

"How did we get in here?" I asked.

"The ocean water formed a canal like a ditch to lead us in here. We are safe. We use this volcano quite often. We get our energy here."

"What do you mean?" I asked, trying to figure out how that could work.

"We mine the coal out of the rock," Captain Nemo said. "That is how we get our power."

It was funny. I had never really thought of that before. Now that I knew about this place, and about how the beast kept going, it was a wonderful addition to the story of the submarine.

"We will be working here today," the captain said. "If you and your friends would like to look around the cavern, you may go ahead."

I thanked the captain and went to look for Ned and Conseil. As I did, I wondered if Captain Nemo had any idea how much Ned wanted to leave. Did he know we were planning an escape? Was he going to have his own plan for keeping us away from land to make our try impossible?

I invited my two friends to follow me without telling them where we were going. It was hard to surprise Conseil with anything, for he was always one step ahead of me. That's the way it was today. And Ned, rather than enjoying the day, thought of nothing other than finding out if we could get off the mountain through the cavern.

Despite the fact that they didn't share my

feelings of excitement, we spent the rest of the day exploring. As we climbed on board the *Nautilus* at the end of the day, we saw that the crew had just finished loading the coal. The ship could have left right then, but Captain Nemo gave no order. Did he want to wait until tonight and leave secretly in the dark? Was this just in case we did try to sneak away? Perhaps so. Whatever it was, the next day the *Nautilus* steered clear of all land. It made me wonder about the captain even more.

For nineteen days the *Nautilus* stayed in the middle of the Atlantic, carrying us at a speed of one hundred leagues a day. Nothing of any importance happened during this long time. However, Ned seemed to grow angrier by the day. It was as if the captain was purposely trying to keep the ship in the middle of the waters.

By March 13th, we had traveled about thirteen thousand leagues since our departure in the Pacific. My companions came to me in my room.

"I have a simple question to ask you," Ned said.

"Speak, Ned."

"How many men do you think there are on board the *Nautilus*?"

"I can't tell, my friend," I said.

"I would say that the jobs here do not need a large crew."

"I agree," I said. "I would say ten men at the most."

I let Ned talk on for a bit about how much air each man used up on the *Nautilus* each day and how many men could survive for certain amounts of time. I did feel sorry for the man. He must be so unhappy here on the ship. I still wasn't sorry enough to make my feelings match his. I was quite happy on the *Nautilus* and looked forward to tomorrow already.

CHAPTER 16

The Hunt

〜

As the days went by and Ned's plan to escape never happened, I began to grow more and more sorry for my friend. Very little interested him. He didn't study the seas like the captain and I did. There was hardly anything that excited him. But on this one particular day, an event occurred that, be it good or bad, did cause the man much excitement.

About eleven in the morning, as we were seated on the platform, the *Nautilus* fell in with a troop of whales.

"Ah!" exclaimed Ned, "if I were on board a whaler boat now, it would be so great! That whale is so large! See the air and steam coming up through its blow-holes? Why do I have to be here? Why?"

I watched my friend as he walked around the platform, following the sights on the horizon.

"They are coming nearer!" Ned exclaimed. "I can see twenty—maybe more! Oh, I am not able to do anything!"

"Ned," I said, stepping up to watch the whales. "Why don't you just ask Captain Nemo if you could chase them?"

For the first time in a long time, I saw a sparkle in Ned's eyes. Before I could say another word he had lowered himself through the panel to find the captain. A few minutes later, they both appeared on the platform.

"I see. They are southern whales," the captain said.

"Can I chase them? It would remind me so much of my days of harpooning!" Ned was almost begging the captain.

"For what?" Captain Nemo asked. "Just to destroy them? We have nothing to do with whale-oil on board. It would be killing for killing's sake."

The captain went on about the endangered animals of the world, those killed for pleasure only. I could see Ned, his back turned, trying to tune out his voice. It was easy to see he was hurt. He knew what the captain was saying was true. And yet he still wanted to continue the sport. He was a man wishing at this moment he was anywhere but here.

"Wait!" the captain said, changing the tone in his voice. "Do you see, behind the whales, about eight miles or so, there is something moving?"

"Yes, Captain," I replied.

"Those are cachalots—terrible animals.

They are mean and cruel beasts. It would only be right to kill *them*."

Ned turned quickly at his words.

"Can we …?"

"The *Nautilus* will take care of them," the captain said. "We have a steel spear that will match any of your harpoons, Mr. Land."

The two men talked back and forth, then agreed to go to the whales' assistance. The *Nautilus* went underwater. Conseil, Ned, and I took our places in front of the window in the saloon. Captain Nemo joined his pilot to work the engine.

The battle between the whales and their enemies had already started. But when our vessel joined in—what a battle! The steel blade of the ship wiped out the animals one by one. A few of the nasty-mouthed beasts tried to attack the *Nautilus*. Ned shouted at them as they struck the side of our vessel over and over. Within a short amount of time, though, the animals were all left for dead.

"This was hunting?" Ned said in anger. "This was more like a butcher using his knife. I like my harpoon better."

"To each his own," the captain said.

From that day forward, I saw in Ned a new sense of hate for our leader. I hoped daily that a fight would not break out. I made it my job to keep my friend under control.

CHAPTER 17

The South Pole

∽

About eight o'clock on the morning of the 16th of March, the *Nautilus* entered the Antarctic polar circle. Ice surrounded us on all sides. I can't describe the beauty of what we saw. The ice was in such surprising shapes. Occasionally I would panic, thinking we were trapped inside the icy forts. But Captain Nemo always discovered a way out. On this day, however, the ice truly blocked our road. It was not so much the iceberg itself, but a field of coldness that wouldn't let us through.

But Captain Nemo wasn't about to stop. He kept forcing the ship against the iceberg. For two days the captain rammed the ice. Ice pellets were thrown high into the air. It fell like hail around us. But the mass of ice would not move.

I was on the platform that night. Captain Nemo had been thinking about our situation for some time when he said to me, "Well, sir, what do you think of this?"

"I think we are stuck, Captain."

"So, Mr. Aronnax, you really think that the *Nautilus* cannot move?" the captain asked, looking for honesty.

"Perhaps it could move," I said, "but not without great difficulty."

The captain answered, "Personally, I think the ship can get out and can go even farther still."

"Farther to the south?" I asked, looking at the captain.

"Yes, sir, it shall go to the pole."

"To the pole?" I asked, sounding like an excited child.

"Yes," replied the captain coldly, "to the Antarctic pole."

I got caught up in the excitement of our talk. "Let's go ahead!" I cried. "Let nothing stand in our way! Let us smash up this iceberg! Let us blow it up, and if it doesn't work, we'll give the *Nautilus* wings to fly over it!"

"No, not over it, sir!" said Captain Nemo quietly. "Not *over* it, but *under* it!"

"Under it!" I yelled. I understood.

"I see we are starting to think alike," said Captain Nemo, smiling. "You are beginning to see the possibilities. Things that are impossible with an ordinary ship are easy for the *Nautilus*."

We discussed for the next several moments the problems that we could meet in the hours to come.

"The only big problem I see," said Captain Nemo, "is that of being under the iceberg for days without coming up to get air." Of course this would be a life-or-death problem, one that needed careful planning. But by four o'clock that afternoon, Captain Nemo called for the closing of the platform. I took one last look at the huge iceberg we were going to cross.

For a part of the night, we kept watch out the window. The sea was lit by the electric lanterns, but there was no ocean life present. We moved quickly. By about two in the morning, I went to sleep.

The next morning, the 19th of March, I went to the saloon to check on the past hours' work. The instrument told me our speed had dropped way down. We were moving toward the surface. My heart began to beat fast. A shock told me that the *Nautilus* had struck the bottom of the iceberg. There were still about three thousand feet of ice above us.

Several times that day, the *Nautilus* tried again and again. It wasn't even close to breaking through such a mass of ice.

It was now time to begin worrying about the oxygen on board. Our air supply should have been refilled four hours ago. I didn't suffer much, but Captain Nemo still had no plan on exactly when to use the extra oxygen he had stored on board.

My sleep was painful that night. I tossed and turned. I awoke several times. In the middle of the night, I noticed that the *Nautilus* was only fifty feet under the iceberg. I watched the instrument as it kept telling us that we were rising closer and closer toward the surface of the ocean. We could see the gleaming of the sun through the ice before we were actually at the top. What a wonderful sight it was to see. At six o'clock in the morning, Captain Nemo appeared at the door.

"The sea is open!" was all he said.

I rushed onto the platform. Yes! The open sea, with just a few scattered pieces of ice and moving icebergs—a long stretch of sea, a world of birds in the air, and fishes of all colors under those waters. It seemed like spring the way we were shut up behind this iceberg.

"Are we at the pole?" I asked the captain with a fast-beating heart.

"I don't know," he replied. "At noon I will take our readings with the sun."

"But do you think the sun will show itself through this fog?" I said.

"It will be fine," Captain Nemo answered.

By ten A.M., we were ready for a visit to the island. We took the rowboat to shore. Conseil was going to jump onto the land, when I held him back.

"Sir," said I to Captain Nemo, "you are the one who deserves to be first upon this land."

"Yes," said the captain. We could tell he liked

119

the attention. He gazed at the island as though he'd never really seen it before. "Until this time, no human being has stepped foot on the South Pole."

He jumped lightly onto the sand. He climbed a rock, crossed his arms, and gazed out over the land. He looked like a king who had just returned to his own kingdom. After about five minutes, he finally turned to us and invited us onto the land.

The rest of us joined him. I couldn't wait to explore! I didn't know where to start first.

My feet made my mind up for me. The soil I was walking on was made of a reddish, sandy stone. It had been made by a volcano. There was little plant life in this area. Most of it was tiny bits washed up from the sea. As for animal life, there were some species of little mussels and sea-butterflies and mollusks. The most dramatic thing I noticed, though, was the wonderful example of life in the air. Thousands of birds fluttered and flew. Their cries were so loud we could hear nothing else. Others crowded onto rocks, looking at us as we passed by. They hopped about our feet without fear. There were penguins, graceful in the water despite how funny they looked on land. They were uttering loud cries. We watched as different species flew, swam, and walked about us. I stood in amazement as I tried to recall these birds from the many bird species books I'd read. Chionis, albatrosses, petrels, and damiers came to mind. It was hard to believe they were actually in front of me, allowing me to study them up close.

It was hard to believe there could be any disappointment on this day. But there was. The fog did not lift and the sun did not appear. We could not know for sure that we were actually on the pole. To make it worse, the white fog turned to snow.

"Until tomorrow," said the captain quietly.

We returned to the *Nautilus* with mixed feelings. We felt great joy at the wonders we had seen, but still a sadness that we did not find the truth.

The snow continued into the next day. It was impossible to stay on the platform. From the window in the saloon where I was taking notes, I could hear the cries of birds in the storm. The *Nautilus* did not remain still, but went up the coast about ten miles.

By the next day, the 20th of March, the snow had stopped. It was a little colder—the thermometer reading two degrees above zero. The fog was rising. There was hope for the sun. Captain Nemo wasn't there, so Conseil and I took the boat to the island ourselves. The soil was the same as it had been on our last stop, but the birds now shared their land with large troops of sea-mammals. They looked at us with their soft eyes. There were several kinds of seals, some stretched on the earth, some on the ice, many going in and out of the sea.

They did not leave as we got closer. I was surprised, since they had never seen men before.

Conseil and I spent the next three hours studying and watching these mammals. What pleasure we found! Just to listen to them, watch them play, feel their skin…I could have spent days with these curious creatures.

At ten o'clock we decided to head back and see if Captain Nemo had found good conditions to get a report on where we were. We took a different path back to the starting point. The boat had gone back for the captain. I saw him standing there, looking toward the sky. We would need the highest point for true readings to appear.

The captain and I went alone to check the instruments. We climbed the steep slope for two hours to reach the highest point. The captain set up his tools and set his sights on the sun.

"It is twelve o'clock," I exclaimed. We held our breath as the instrument measured.

"The South Pole!" replied Captain Nemo in a serious voice.

I looked at the man who had tried so hard to find this land. At that moment Captain Nemo, resting with his hand on my shoulder, said:

"I, Captain Nemo, on this 21st day of March, 1868, have reached the South Pole. I now take possession of this part of the globe, equal to one-sixth of the known continents."

"In whose name, Captain?"

"In my own, sir!"

Captain Nemo unrolled a black flag with a gold letter N.

As we placed the flag into the snowy ice and cold, we saw the sun begin to disappear beneath the open sea. Six months of night was spreading its shadows over the captain's new land.

CHAPTER 18

Stranded

৵

At six o'clock the next morning, the 22nd of March, we began to get ready to leave. The last bits of light were melting into night. The cold was great and the stars hung low above us.

Our trip began. We went down a thousand feet and went north at a speed of fifteen miles an hour. Toward night we began our way under the iceberg. At three in the morning I was woken up by a violent shock. I sat up in my bed and listened in the darkness. Suddenly I was thrown into the middle of the room. The *Nautilus*, having been hit, jerked strongly. I felt my way along the wall and followed the staircase to the saloon. The furniture was turned over. The pictures on the walls were crooked. The *Nautilus* was lying on its side, perfectly still. I heard footsteps and voices but Captain Nemo didn't appear. As I was leaving the saloon, Ned and Conseil entered.

"What is the matter?" I asked at once.

"I came to ask you, sir," replied Conseil.

"I know," Ned said. "The *Nautilus* has hit something. And by the way she is lying, I don't think she is going to right herself this time!"

"Are we at the surface?" I asked.

"We don't know," said Conseil.

"It's easy to find out," I said. I went over to the manometer. This tool showed us how deep we were. To my great surprise, it showed that we were more than a hundred and eighty fathoms down. "What does that mean?" I exclaimed.

"We must ask Captain Nemo," said Conseil.

"But where is he?" said Ned.

"Follow me," I said to my companions.

We left the saloon. There was no one in the library, the staircase, or the pilot's cage. We returned to the saloon. For twenty minutes we waited, listening for the smallest noise. Finally, Captain Nemo entered. He acted as if he didn't even see us. His face, usually so proud, showed signs of worry. He watched the compass, then the manometer, then the other instruments he used to guide the ship. I didn't interrupt him, but was glad when he finally turned toward me.

"Something's happened, Captain?" I asked.

"Yes, an accident."

"Serious?" I asked.

"Maybe," the captain answered.

"Are we in danger right at this moment?"

"No," he answered.

"Are we stuck here?" I asked, hoping for the right answer.

"Yes, we are stranded."

"But how?" I asked. "How did this happen?"

"It wasn't anyone's fault," the captain answered. It happened because of science—the way the ocean is working."

The captain went on to explain the details. A mountain of ice had turned over. When it fell, it hit the *Nautilus*, causing it to turn on its side. The *Nautilus* was slowly rising, but the mountain of ice was rising with the ship. The ship could continue to rise until it hit the surface and fixed itself, or…the ship could be crushed between two mountains of ice.

Captain Nemo never took his eyes off the manometer. The *Nautilus* had risen about a hundred and fifty feet since he had first looked at it. Suddenly we felt a slight movement. Pictures hanging in the saloon were returning to their normal position. No one spoke. With beating hearts we watched and felt the *Nautilus* straighten. A slow ten minutes passed.

"At last we have righted!" I exclaimed. "But are we floating?"

"Certainly," Captain Nemo replied. We went down the hall and climbed the steps leading to the gate. We stepped out onto the platform to see an amazing sight. We were in open sea, but with a dazzling wall of ice around us. In fact, we were in a perfect tunnel of ice. It was easy to get out of it by going either forward or backward, and then going under the iceberg a hundred yards or so.

The next few moments were dazzling. The shine made by the ice actually hurt our eyes. It took some time at last to calm down.

It was then five in the morning. At that moment we felt a shock. I knew right away that we had hit a block of ice. I also knew that Captain Nemo would simply find another turn in the tunnel. Instead, I felt the *Nautilus* start backward.

"That's no problem," I thought out loud. "We will just go back out and go to the southern opening."

But hours passed. I stayed with my friends to make the waiting seem better. I kept looking at the long instruments hanging in the saloon. We were still more than three hundred feet down. We were still moving south and we were traveling at a speed of twenty miles an hour. But Captain Nemo knew what he was doing. I tried not to worry.

At twenty-five minutes past eight, a second shock took place. This time it came from behind. I turned pale. My friends were close by my side. I took Conseil's hand and squeezed it. The looks on our faces told more than words. At this moment, the captain entered the saloon. I walked up to him.

"Our path is now blocked in the south?" I asked.

"Yes. The iceberg has moved and every open spot is now blocked."

"We are trapped?" I whispered.

"Yes. Yes we are."

CHAPTER 19

Air Supply

Around the *Nautilus*, above and below, was a thick wall of ice. We were prisoners to the iceberg. I watched the captain. His face showed some concern.

"Gentlemen," he said calmly, "I fear you are worrying about things that need not be." The confused looks we gave him told him to continue.

"First, we would never starve to death on this ship. There are enough food supplies on this vessel to outlast any disaster."

I had not thought about this, so it didn't make me feel any better to hear it.

"Second, I know you have all thought about the possibility of running out of air. This should not be feared. We have a supply of air on board for forty-eight hours."

"But, Captain, what happens after that time?" I asked.

"I think, sir, we shall be through that wall of ice by then."

"On which side?" I asked.

"I will use my tools to find the thinnest side. My men will attack the iceberg there."

I knew the third option that we should fear. Being crushed under a mound of ice was always on my mind. I didn't need him to remind me.

Captain Nemo went out. I felt the ship sink slowly and rest on the ice at a depth of three hundred and fifty yards.

"My friends," I said, "our situation is serious. But I know you will show me courage."

Every person on board was ready to show that courage. We prepared ourselves in cork-jackets. A dozen of the crew at a time stepped out on the bank of ice with their pickaxes. After two hours' hard work, Ned and the others came in exhausted. He and that crew were replaced with new workers whom Conseil and I joined. The water seemed very cold, but I soon got warm from swinging the ax. When I went back into the *Nautilus* to get some food and rest, I found a big difference in the air. It was harder to breathe in the ship. The air had not been refreshed in two days. Already I could feel the difference. I shivered, thinking about the hours to come. After twelve hours of work, we had only broken through one yard of the ice! At this pace it would take five nights and four days to break through completely. But we only had air enough for two days on the ship! We would run out of air long before the *Nautilus* could ever get to the surface.

We all kept up our work without complaining or thinking of the awful things that could lie ahead. At least when you were swinging the pickax, you felt as if you were helping. You also felt as if you were alive. This was where the breathable air was. These were the men who needed the pure air most. When one went for break inside the vessel, it was hard to believe the difference in the air. I could hardly catch my breath. The chemicals we breathed out had no place to go within the ship. We were simply breathing our own air back in. There should have been some pure air pumped into the *Nautilus*, but this was not possible.

For days, we lived with the fact that the air was slowly being taken away from us. The men continued to dig in shifts to break through the ice wall. Of course we had slowed down. Our bodies were weak and our only thoughts were of air. Captain Nemo was forced to think beyond his original plan. Even in his sorry condition, the man thought quickly and came up with bright ideas.

One of his tricks was to use jets of boiling water to raise the temperature in this part of the sea. Another action, which probably saved our lives in the end, was to lighten the ship. He then filled its storage area with water. The weight of the *Nautilus* was now eighteen hundred tons. The ice beneath us cracked and the ship sank. The pumps soon began to let the water out of the ship. As it got lighter, the *Nautilus* began to move at a very fast pace. It tore through the water, shooting forward like a bullet onto the icy field. We blasted through to the surface and tasted the salty sea air that we had been dreaming about for days. That was the closest I ever came to dying.

CHAPTER 20

The Final Escape

︾

For seven months, we had been prisoners on board the *Nautilus*. We had traveled seventeen thousand leagues. Ned finally said, "There is no reason why it shouldn't come to an end."

Besides, Captain Nemo seemed to have changed lately. He wasn't as friendly or as helpful as he once was. He even seemed to ignore me. I rarely saw him. It used to be that when he found something exciting in his studies he would rush to share it with me. Now he left me to my studies and never came to the saloon. What caused this change?

There had been one terrible night in April that none of us would ever forget. A giant poulp, a fish more like a monster than a sea animal, had attacked our ship and killed one of our crew. This man was a good friend of Captain Nemo. I saw him crying more than once as he looked out over the waves.

It was also at this time that Ned came to me with a strong request.

"Professor," he said to me, "this must come to an end. Nemo is leaving land and going up to the north. But, I tell you, I have had enough of the South Pole. I will not follow him to the North."

"What are you going to do, Ned?"

"There are some places I could reach before we get too far," Ned said. "But no matter. I will throw myself in the sea before continuing on this trip! You must talk to him!"

I knew how serious Ned was. I was feeling more and more like him every day. I gave myself an hour then went to see the captain.

"But we have been here seven months!" I said when the captain gave me a stern "no" right from the beginning.

"I told you that whoever enters the *Nautilus* must never leave it," snapped the captain.

We argued for a few minutes. It was pointless. I knew I would get nowhere. I told Ned we would have to plan our secret escape. We could wait no longer. The flight would be tonight, no matter what the weather was like.

But the sky became more and more threatening. Signs of a hurricane began. Winds, fierce rains, and violent thunder and lightning rocked the ship.

"We can still make it!" Ned said. As dangerous as it seemed, I decided to take the risk with him. I gathered my notes, walked nervously through the saloon where the captain was, and went up onto the platform. The driving rain forced us back inside for a few minutes to talk. As we began our conversation, I felt the doors on the platform click and seal. Within seconds, I felt the *Nautilus* begin to sink. Once again our escape had been spoiled.

The disappointment we felt made us sick. If what happened next hadn't happened, I think Ned would have jumped right into the icy water. For a quarter of an hour we watched a ship that was coming toward us. When it got close enough for us to feel hope, the shooting of guns brought fear and anger.

"Why are they firing at us?" Ned cried.

"It doesn't really matter," the captain said coldly. "They are asking for a fight."

But for whatever reason, Captain Nemo stopped himself from firing right then. My friends and I all went to our cabins for the night.

Most of the evening passed without any action. At three in the morning, very nervous, I went to the platform. Captain Nemo had not left it. It took hours, but the captain finally did destroy the ship. As awful as it was, I almost wished I could have been there taking my chances in the fight with them.

In the days to come, I actually lost track of time. I didn't know our speed or our location. We drifted and I didn't care where. I was becoming more and more like my friends. I wanted to get off the ship.

"We are leaving tonight!" Ned said early one morning.

We weren't sure of the country, the distance, or the weather, but we had promised ourselves that tonight was the night. My next hours were hard. I wanted to go to Captain Nemo and thank him. I wanted to let him know that I would never forget my time on his ship. But I also knew he would never let us off this ship alive. Instead, I spent the time until ten o'clock in my room.

At ten, I crept along the carpet in the hall and turned the saloon door quietly. Captain Nemo was sitting near the instruments. I had no choice. I had to go near him. As I did, he turned around. I could have sworn he had tears in his eyes. I wanted to reach out to him, but I couldn't. Instead, I rushed through the library, up the staircase, out the door, and into the small rowboat kept on board. I felt sure that the captain was not following me.

"Let's go! Let's go!" I exclaimed.

It was awful! The waves were rocking our boat up and down. The noise was loud enough that we couldn't hear one another talk. Letting go of the *Nautilus* and allowing our little boat to go free in the middle of the ocean seemed stupid at this point. But getting back out and facing the captain, who would surely be angry, seemed just as stupid.

We really had no choice. My companions were trying to come up with ideas when a piece of iron struck me on the head. I passed out on the boat, not knowing where the next few hours took me.

When I came to, I was lying in a fisherman's hut. My two companions were near me, safe and sound, holding my hands. We hugged one another tightly.

I laid my head back on the pillow and smiled. Would anyone believe the adventure we had just been on? Really . . . it didn't matter. I have earned the right to speak of these seas. After all, in less

than ten months, I had crossed twenty thousand leagues in a submarine tour of the world.

But what became of the *Nautilus*? Where is Captain Nemo? Will the waves one day carry to him the book I've written about him? Will I ever learn all the answers to the questions I have about this man?

I hope so. I also hope that his powerful ship survives where others have failed. May goodness be spread to his heart from the wonders he finds. I pray he finds peace in his study of the sea.

After spending nine months with Captain Nemo in the world beneath the ocean, did we find the answers to all of life's questions? Probably not. But do we have the right to present our findings to make the world a better place? Time shall tell. I only know I experienced a time like no other. I learned more from this man than any school could have taught me. I was a prisoner, but a willing one. I respect this man and thank him for the gift he has given me.

That which is far off and very deep, who can find out? Two men alone now have that right to give the answer—CAPTAIN NEMO AND MYSELF.

What Do *You* Think?
Questions for Discussion

ℭ

Have you ever been around a toddler who keeps asking the question "Why?" Does your teacher call on you in class with questions from your homework? Do your parents ask you questions about your day at the dinner table? We are always surrounded by questions that need a specific response. But is it possible to have a question with no right answer?

The following questions are about the book you just read. But this is not a quiz! They are designed to help you look at the people, places, and events in the story from different angles. These questions do not have specific answers. Instead, they might make you think of the story in a completely new way.

Think carefully about each question and enjoy discovering more about this classic story.

1. When he first hears about the mysterious creature, Professor Aronnax says that it must be either a narwhal or a boat. Did you come up with any other possibilities? Were you surprised to discover that it was a submarine? Have you ever been involved in unraveling a mystery?

2. Why do you suppose Conseil jumps into the water after Professor Aronnax? Have you ever done something dangerous to help a friend? What was it?

3. Captain Nemo says that the sea makes him feel safe from all the harms in the world. Why do you think he feels this way? Where do you go to feel safe?

4. How do you think Captain Nemo has changed as a result of living underwater for so long? What kind of man do you suppose he was before creating the *Nautilus*? Have you ever known anyone like Captain Nemo?

5. On one of their many adventures, Captain Nemo takes Professor Aronnax to see Atlantis. Do you believe this city actually exists? What do you suppose we would see if we actually found it?

6. Arronax is torn between gaining his freedom and leaving the *Nautilus*. Why does he make the choice he does? What would you have done in his position?

7. Why do you think Captain Nemo is so eager to discover the South Pole? Have you ever discovered anything yourself?

8. Do you think Captain Nemo is a hero or a villain? Why?

9. When Aronnax is called in to look at one of the men's wounds, he hesitates to tell Captain

Nemo that the man is dying. Have you ever had to deliver bad news? How did you do it?

10. Many of the tools that Verne writes about had not yet been invented when the book was written. If you were writing a similar book today, what would you invent?

Afterword

by Arthur Pober, EdD

⤫

First impressions are important.

Whether we are meeting new people, going to new places, or picking up a book unknown to us, first impressions count for a lot. They can lead to warm, lasting memories or can make us shy away from any future encounters.

Can you recall your own first impressions and earliest memories of reading the classics?

Do you remember wading through pages and pages of text to prepare for an exam? Or were you the child who hid under the blanket to read with a flashlight, joining forces with Robin Hood to save Maid Marian? Do you remember only how long it took you to read a lengthy novel such as *Little Women*? Or did you become best friends with the March sisters?

Even for a gifted young reader, getting through long chapters with dense language can easily become overwhelming and can obscure the richness of the story and its characters. Reading an abridged, newly crafted version of a classic novel can be the gentle introduction a child needs to explore the characters and story line without the frustration of difficult vocabulary and complex themes.

Reading an abridged version of a classic novel gives the young reader a sense of independence and the satisfaction of finishing a "grown-up" book. And when a child is engaged with and inspired by a classic story, the tone is set for further exploration of the story's themes, characters, history, and details. As a child's reading skills advance, the desire to tackle the original, unabridged version of the story will naturally emerge.

If made accessible to young readers, these stories can become invaluable tools for understanding themselves in the context of their families and social environments. This is why the *Classic Starts* series includes questions that stimulate discussion regarding the impact and social relevance of the characters and stories today. These questions can foster lively conversations between children and their parents or teachers. When we look at the issues, values, and standards of past times in terms of how we live now, we can appreciate literature's classic tales in a very personal and engaging way.

Share your love of reading the classics with a young child, and introduce an imaginary world real enough to last a lifetime.

Dr. Arthur Pober, EdD

Dr. Arthur Pober has spent more than twenty years in the fields of early-childhood and gifted education. He is the former principal of one of the world's oldest laboratory schools for gifted youngsters, Hunter College Elementary School, and former director of Magnet Schools for the Gifted and Talented for more than 25,000 youngsters in New York City.

Dr. Pober is a recognized authority in the areas of media and child protection and is currently the U.S. representative to the European Institute for the Media and European Advertising Standards Alliance.

Explore these wonderful stories in our
Classic Starts™ library.